Wild About Books

by JUDY SIERRA

pictures by MARC BROWN

Alfred A. Knopf   New York

It started the summer of 2002,
When the Springfield librarian, Molly McGrew,
By mistake drove her bookmobile into the zoo.
Molly opened the door, and she let down the stair,
Turned on the computer, and sat in her chair.

At first all the animals watched from a distance,
But Molly could conquer the strongest resistance.

By reading aloud from the good Dr. Seuss,
She quickly attracted a mink and a moose,
A wombat, an oryx, a lemur, a lynx,
Eight elephant calves, and a family of skinks.

In a flash, every beast in the zoo was stampeding
To learn all about this new something called *reading*.

Forsaking their niches, their nests, and their nooks,
They went wild, simply wild, about wonderful books,
Choosing thin books and fat books and Cat in the Hat books
And new books and true books and heaps of how-to books.

Giraffes wanted tall books and crickets craved small books,
While geckos could only read stick-to-the-wall books.

The pandas demanded more books in Chinese.
Molly filled their requests, always eager to please.
She even found waterproof books for the otter,
Who never went swimming without *Harry Potter*.

Raccoons read alone and baboons read in bunches.
And llamas read dramas while eating their llunches.

Hyenas shared jokes with the red-bellied snakes,
And they howled and they hissed till their funny bones ached.

A tree kangaroo, who adored *Nancy Drew*,
Began solving mysteries right there at the zoo,
Such as, Why were the bandicoot's books overdue?

Gently, Molly taught lessons in treating books right,

For the boa constrictor squeezed *Crictor* too tight,

Baby bunnies mucked up *Goodnight Moon* with their paws,

Giant termites devoured *The Wizard of Oz*,

And bears' love of books was completely outrageous—
They licked all the pictures right off of the pages.

Raccoons read alone and baboons read in bunches.

And llamas read dramas while eating their llunches.

Hyenas shared jokes with the red-bellied snakes,
And they howled and they hissed till their funny bones ached.

A tree kangaroo, who adored *Nancy Drew*,
Began solving mysteries right there at the zoo,
Such as, Why were the bandicoot's books overdue?

Gently, Molly taught lessons in treating books right,
For the boa constrictor squeezed *Crictor* too tight,
Baby bunnies mucked up *Goodnight Moon* with their paws,
Giant termites devoured *The Wizard of Oz*,

And bears' love of books was completely outrageous—
They licked all the pictures right off of the pages.

BIG BAD
BRUCE

Tasmanian devils found books so exciting
That soon they had given up fighting for writing.
They made up adventures so thrilling and new
That the others decided to be authors, too.
Pythons wrote with their tails, penguins wrote with their bills,
And porcupines wrote with their very own quills.

At the new insect zoo, bugs were scribbling haiku.
(The scorpion gave each a stinging review.)

Walking Stick

A cannibal twig
Silently devours a leaf—
Eating, not eaten.

Pretentious.

Dung Beetle

Roll a ball of dung—
Any kind of poo will do—
Baby beetle bed.

Stinks.

It was a dark and stormy night. The wind howled. The moon cast a mournful pale yellow glow. bags waited in the dark b...

As the cheetah's new novel began to take shape,
He read chapters each night to the Barbary ape;
And although the gazelle couldn't spell very well,
Like everyone else, she had stories to tell.

Imagine the hippo's enormous surprise
When her memoir was given the Zoolitzer Prize.

With so many new books, Molly knew what to do—
She hired twelve beavers, a stork, and a gnu
To build a branch library there at the zoo.
Then the animals cried, "We can do it ourselves!
We can check the books out. We can put them on shelves."

And they did, and they do, up to this very day.
Three cheers for the Zoobrary—

Hip, hip, hooray!

When you visit the zoo now, you surely won't mind
If the animals seem just a bit hard to find—
They are snug in their niches, their nests, and their nooks,
Going wild, simply wild, about wonderful books.

THIS IS A BORZOI BOOK PUBLISHED BY ALFRED A. KNOPF

Text copyright © 2004 by Judy Sierra

Illustrations copyright © 2004 by Marc Brown

All rights reserved under International and Pan-American Copyright Conventions. Published in the United States by
Alfred A. Knopf, an imprint of Random House Children's Books, a division of Random House, Inc., New York, and simultaneously in
Canada by Random House of Canada Limited, Toronto. Distributed by Random House, Inc., New York.

KNOPF, BORZOI BOOKS, and the colophon are registered trademarks of Random House, Inc.

www.randomhouse.com/kids

Library of Congress Cataloging-in-Publication Data

Sierra, Judy.

Wild about books / by Judy Sierra ; illustrated by Marc Brown. — 1st ed.

p.   cm.

SUMMARY: A librarian named Molly McGrew introduces the animals in the zoo to the joy of reading when she drives her bookmobile
to the zoo by mistake.

ISBN 0-375-82538-X (trade) — ISBN 0-375-92538-4 (lib. bdg.)

[1. Zoo animals—Fiction. 2. Books and reading—Fiction. 3. Bookmobiles—Fiction. 4. Libraries—Fiction. 5. Stories in rhyme.]

I. Brown, Marc Tolon, ill. II. Title.

PZ8.3.S577Wi 2004

[E]—dc21

2003008135

MANUFACTURED IN THE U.S.A.

August 2004

16 15 14 13

First Edition

This book is for our favorite doctor,
artist, poet, fun concocter:
Theodor Seuss Geisel, 1904–1991.

—Judy Sierra and Marc Brown

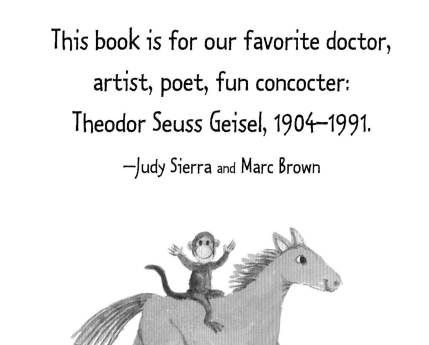